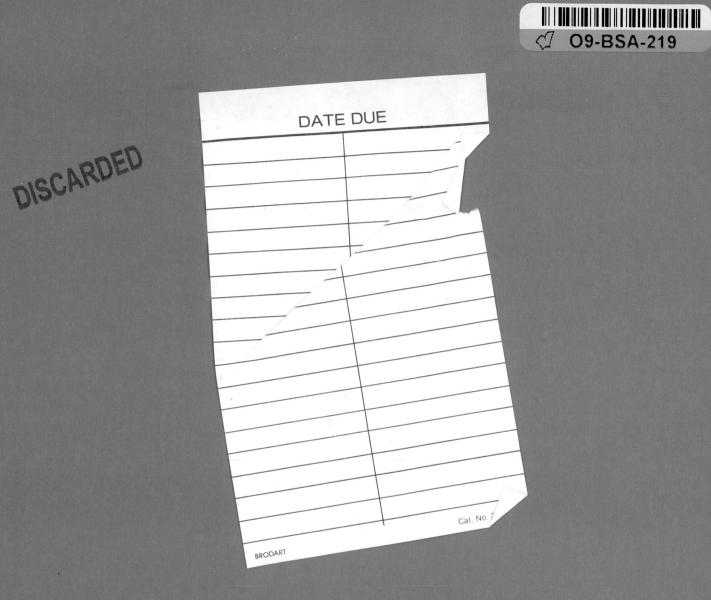

DATE DUE

BRODART

Cat. No.

For Simon

Illustrations copyright © 1999 by Alison Jay
Text copyright © 1999 by The Templar Company plc
All rights reserved.
CIP Data is available.
Published in the United States 2000 by Dutton Children's Books,
a division of Penguin Putnam Books for Young Readers
345 Hudson Street, New York, New York 10014
First published in the UK 1999 by Templar Publishing,
an imprint of The Templar Company plc, Surrey
Concept by Dugald Steer
Printed in Belgium
First American Edition
ISBN 0-525-46380-1
1 3 5 7 9 8 6 4 2

Picture This

ALISON JAY

Dutton Children's Books • New York

clock

dog

hill

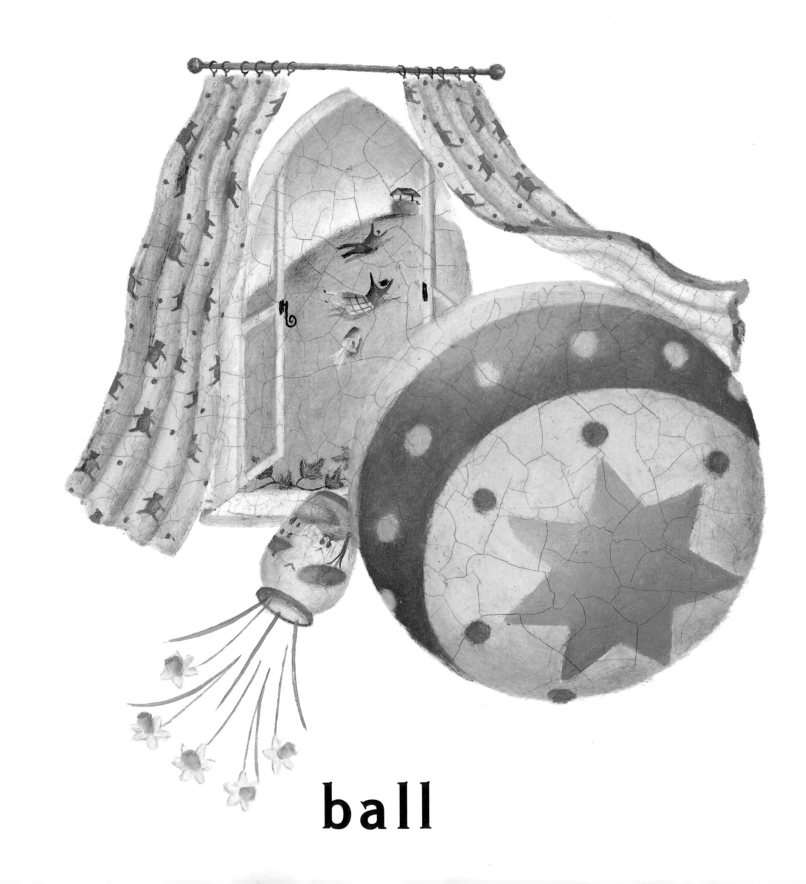

ball

teddy bear

hat

fish

house

toy box

flower

cat

airplane

kite

sand castle

ship

car

tortoise

leaf

snail

boots

umbrella

books

bed

train

cake

snowman